THE RAGING TORRENT

D1375443

GLADIATOR BOY

Win an exclusive
Gladiator Boy T-shirt and goody bag!

Use the special code below to decode the sentence, then send it in to us.
Each month we will draw one winner to receive a Gladiator Boy T-shirt
and goody bag.

Send your entry on a postcard to:
GLADIATOR BOY: ESCAPE FROM THE EAST COMPETITION,
Hodder Children's Books, 338 Euston Road, London NW1 3BH

Only one entry per child.
Final Draw: 31 December 2010

You can also enter this competition via the Gladiator Boy website
WWW.GLADIATORBOY.COM

THE RAGING TORRENT

DAVID GRIMSTONE

Hodder
Children's
Books

A division of Hachette Children's Books

ISBN: 978 0 340 98928 9

Typeset by Tony Fleetwood

Printed and bound in Great Britain by CPI Bookmarque, Croydon, CR0 4TD

The paper and board used in this paperback by Hodder Children's Books are
natural recyclable products made from wood grown in sustainable
forests. The manufacturing processes conform to the
environmental regulations of the country of origin.

Hodder Children's Books
a division of Hachette Children's Books
338 Euston Road, London NW1 3BH
An Hachette UK company

www.hachette.co.uk

For Stuart Jupp, my role-playing soul-mate …
for all the adventures we've had together!

This new series is dedicated to Leilani Sparrow,
who has worked tirelessly with Gladiator Boy
since his arrival. Thanks also to Anne McNeil,
who has stood in my corner since day one.

HOW MANY OF

GLADIATOR
BOY

SERIES ONE HAVE
YOU COLLECTED?

A HERO'S QUEST

ESCAPE FROM EVIL

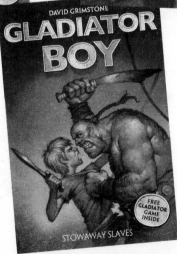

STOWAWAY SLAVES

DAVID GRIMSTONE
GLADIATOR
BOY

THE REBELS' ASSAULT

FREE
GLADIATOR
GAME
INSIDE

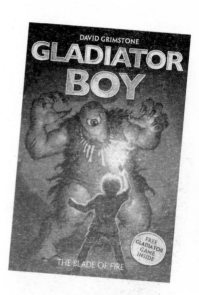

DAVID GRIMSTONE
GLADIATOR
BOY

THE BLADE OF FIRE

FREE
GLADIATOR
GAME
INSIDE

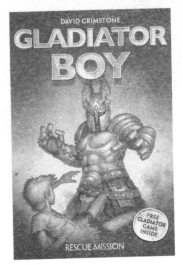

DAVID GRIMSTONE
GLADIATOR
BOY

RESCUE MISSION

FREE
GLADIATOR
GAME
INSIDE

CHINA

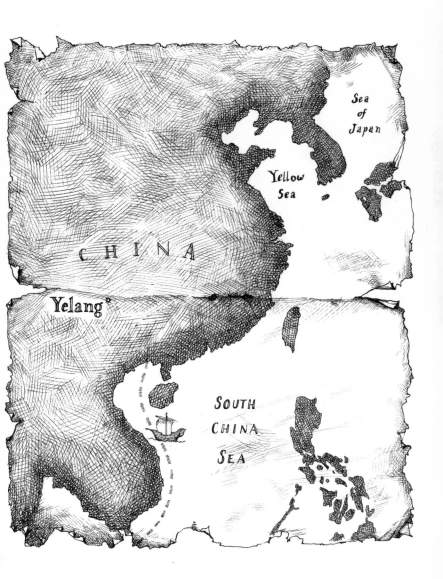

PREVIOUSLY IN GLADIATOR BOY

Decimus and the other slaves are headed to distant China in order to search for Teo, a friend they thought had been murdered by the evil Slavious Doom. Together with an ageing sea captain, they are plotting a course for Yelang, a tiny and very mysterious kingdom in a land they know nothing about . . .

CHAPTER
I

YELANG

L ightning flashed over the ocean, and the booming crack of thunder that followed was so loud it sounded as if the sky was tearing itself apart.

The little schooner carrying Decimus and his friends had been on the seas for almost two months and was drawing near to the coast of China. Tonino had suggested they celebrate with a hearty meal of fish and bread when the first flash of lightning had indicated the arrival of a storm.

At first, the waves had been relatively calm, and even Gladius hadn't panicked too much. Steadily, however, the roar of the thunder increased, the flashes came quicker and the wind cranked up to a twisting, howling gale. Now, they were fighting to stay on their feet, as the storm-tossed sea pitched and hurled the little boat in every direction. One second they were balancing at the top of a high wave, the next they were plunged into a valley of dark water with towering walls of ocean on each side.

Argon, who hated sea-travel at the best of times, had locked himself inside the tiny cabin, while Ruma and Gladius both fought to contain the contents of their stomachs as they clung to the ropes of the giant foresail.

Only Decimus and Olu seemed to have found their sea legs, largely thanks to their great adventure aboard the slave trader. They were valiantly assisting the captain to keep the boat at the top of each charging wave. At the very least, they thought, the sails were holding strong.

Then it happened.

At first, there was just a sickening, ear-splitting crack.

Everyone jumped up, and began to look around for the source of the noise. Only Tonino, who knew every inch of his boat, immediately cast a glance at the mainsail.

It was coming down.

'Run!' he screamed, heading for the port side of the boat. 'Everyone ruuuunnnn!'

Decimus and Olu were both at his side in seconds, and all three took an incredible leap towards the edge of the deck. Behind them, the mainsail literally broke in half, slamming into the deck with a crunch of deafening proportions.

As half of the foredeck crumpled, a single

board shot up and swung around, hitting Ruma in the face and sending him skidding across the ship at an alarming rate. He flew through the air like a dart expelled from a blowpipe, and would undoubtedly have been tossed into the ocean had Argon not chosen that moment to emerge from the captain's cabin.

The door flew open and Ruma cannoned into it, resulting in an explosive shower of wood and water. Amid the collision, Argon was thrown back into the cabin and ended his reverse journey upside down in the captain's hammock.

As a final, heart-ripping clap of thunder signalled the end of the storm, only Gladius remained uninjured. The former slave simply sat on his bottom in the middle of the deck, with a green tinge to his face and two ropes wrapped tightly around him. He looked like a man who'd just survived a raging war and didn't have the slightest clue why. Just as he was about to thank the gods for his luck, however, a barrel lid flew past and clonked him on the head, knocking him out cold.

Slowly, very slowly, the ship began to enter calmer waters.

The storm had passed.

The rest of the journey to China had been an uneventful one. Thankfully, Tonino turned out to be a worthy captain, and had negotiated the rolling waves with a grim determination. The biggest surprise, however, was not the man's skill as a sailor or his detailed knowledge of trading routes, but his generosity. To their complete astonishment, despite the damage his little schooner had suffered during the storm, he'd actually agreed to wait for the group to finish their mission in China before taking them home again. Decimus protested, and even Argon had pointed out that they had little or no idea how long it would be before they returned from Yelang, but Tonino refused to budge. Instead, he made mention of wanting to work on some international trading plan he'd been cooking up, and said he'd look forward to the 'peace and quiet'. The repairs to the sail would take at least a week, he'd assured them.

Eventually, Decimus managed to work out a solution he thought was fair. Olu and Argon would stay and help Tonino to fix his ship, while he, Gladius and Ruma left for Yelang.

Naturally, the idea was greeted with protests.

'You can't go off looking for Teo by yourselves,' Argon snapped, flexing his arm-muscles in an attempt to prove his worth to the team. 'He was my friend, too. Besides, I'm stronger than the rest of you. Do you really want to leave these arms out of any rescue attempt?'

Decimus rolled his eyes.

'Argon, we all know how strong you are,' he muttered. 'What I'm saying is that if I'm right and we are walking into a trap, we'll need two reliable friends to come and find us. You with your strength, and Olu because he's faster over open ground than any of us. Doesn't that make sense?'

Argon gave a defeated sigh, but Olu wasn't sure about the idea.

'How long do we give you?' he asked. 'A day? A week? A month?'

Decimus took a moment to think. 'It's a big

country; just wait as long as you can … we will return.'

There were plenty more growls and grumbles from the two former slaves, but deep down they knew it was a sensible plan. Decimus, Gladius and Ruma headed for the mainland with grim determination on their faces. They didn't look back.

China was far more beautiful than Decimus could ever have imagined. There were plateaus and mountains, lowlands and rivers. In almost every direction there was some scene of great beauty – something you almost wanted to capture in a painting. Something there didn't seem to be, however, was a population.

'The place is deserted,' said Ruma, moodily. 'If only Teo had talked more: we might have some idea of what kind of place his home was and where we are walking to.'

'Well, it's hardly likely to be exactly the same as Italy, is it?' Gladius pointed out, sarcastically. 'And I'm pretty sure we haven't run into anyone because we're not travelling on the road.' He suddenly turned to Decimus. 'Why is that, exactly?' he prompted.

'I told you,' said the young gladiator. 'We can't afford to run into any groups. If we meet soldiers, we'll run the risk of capture and if we meet villagers, we might be welcomed into their community and we just can't be distracted from getting to Yelang.'

'We don't even know where Yelang is,' Ruma pointed out.

Decimus nodded. 'I know that,' he snapped. 'But someone will – we just need to make sure we find the right person.'

'So ideally we're looking for a lone wanderer who isn't intimidated by foreign strangers, speaks our language and just happens to turn up in the middle of nowhere?' Gladius smiled broadly. 'I wonder if the gods might have heard you – look, a caravan!'

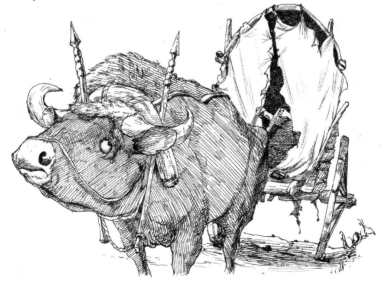

Decimus strained to see the section of path his friend was indicating.

'It's not exactly a lone wanderer,' Gladius went on. 'But it might have to do.'

At first, it looked very much as if the caravan itself was empty. A large ox pulled the rickety little structure, which rattled along the ground and looked as though it might fall to pieces each time the wheels hit a bump in the road.

It wasn't until he drew nearer that Decimus noticed the reins tethering the ox actually disappeared beyond a ragged curtain that concealed the inside of the caravan. Someone was driving the ox, but it didn't look like they could actually see where they were going.

He took a deep breath and stepped out into the middle of the road. The ox took little notice of him, and didn't seem in any mood to stop. If anything, the creature was actually beginning to veer left as if it might move around him.

Casting a glance at the surrounding hills, Decimus tried to see where Gladius and Ruma were hiding. He'd instructed them both to lie in wait at the side of the road to avoid frightening anyone who might be inside. They were awaiting a signal from him.

The young gladiator returned his attention to the road ahead, and yelled at the top of his voice.

'Stop! Halt!'

Almost at once, the reins went taut and the ox slowly stopped moving as it felt its harness tighten. The curtain on the caravan twitched, slightly.

Once.

Twice.

Decimus stepped back as the curtain was wrenched aside. A small, cheerful face peered out at him. It was definitely old, and possibly female, but so crumpled by lines and creases that it was difficult to tell for certain.

'Xìng huì!' said the face in an animated voice. 'Nǐ hǎo!'

Decimus frowned, and raised a hand.

'Hello!' he said, in his least threatening voice.

The little character in the caravan paused for a second, then fully emerged from within.

'Xìng huì!' she repeated.

'Xìng huì!' Decimus called back, taking

28

careful steps towards the caravan. 'I'm afraid I do not speak your language. I'm looking for a map. Hmm...'

While he stood in the middle of the road, trying to think of a physical description he could use, the old woman hurried up to him and made a sudden, unexpected grab for the sword at his side.

'Jīng mào?'

'I don't know what that means.' Decimus held up a warning hand, and took a step back from the old woman. Then he drew out his sword and, turning it around, offered it to the old lady.

However, as she made to snatch the blade once again, he pulled it back and made an expansive gesture with his other hand, indicating the land around her.

'Map!' he said, carefully. Then he crouched down and used his finger to scratch several paths in the dirt before looking up. 'Map?'

The old woman stared at the dirt pattern, and a light seemed to come on behind her eyes.

'Dì tú?' she hazarded. 'Dì tú?'

Without waiting for a reply, she turned and dashed back to the caravan. There was the sound of determined rustling from within, and she reappeared carrying what seemed to be a scroll of some sort. Hurrying up to Decimus, she unfurled the parchment, revealing a detailed plan of a vast and complicated region.

'M-ap,' she confirmed, waving her arm around as he had done before.

Smiling with satisfaction, Decimus handed over the sword . . . but he didn't actually let go of the blade. 'Where are we?' he asked, loudly and clearly, pointing the sword at the ground. 'Where is here?'

The old woman nodded, and jabbed a finger at a point very close to the coast. That made sense; they hadn't yet travelled too far from Tonino's boat.

'Thank you,' said Decimus, gratefully, crouching next to the old woman and placing his sword on the ground beside her. He didn't want to give up his only weapon, but a deal was a deal. 'And now,' he said, finally. 'Where is YELANG on this map? YELANG?'

There was a moment of silence, and the old woman moved her finger a long way north. 'Yelang,' she said, but her expression warned of an unspoken danger.

Yelang was a long way away.

CHAPTER II

THE WINTER PALACE

The trio had been travelling for many days when Decimus spied a familiar-looking symbol on a weathered wooden post.

'That's it,' he said, unfurling the map and matching the symbol on the patch of land the old woman had pointed out to the crude scratching on the post. They were identical.

'Finally,' Ruma muttered. 'We must be getting close.'

Gladius breathed a sigh of exhausted relief.

'Thank the gods for that,' he muttered.

The journey had been arduous. Although the land was outstandingly beautiful, avoiding the various towns and villages was becoming increasingly difficult as the journey progressed. They had adopted a method of hurrying off the road at the first sign of any encounter, which was easily done but happened so often that it became very frustrating. To make matters worse, a cold mist smothered the hills by night, forcing them to huddle for warmth in a makeshift camp between the trees.

The following morning, they reached the Winter Palace. They had spent the early hours negotiating a steep climb up the side of the biggest waterfall Decimus had ever seen in his life. The great rush of water was audible for miles around, and they could still hear it plainly when Ruma caught sight of the palace in the distance.

There could be little doubt that it was the right place. Not only was the palace completely resplendent in the purest white with several pinnacles and covered bridges spanning a number of ornamental waterways, it also boasted a vast, sprawling garden awash with coloured flowers and stone statues in various poses and attitudes. One of these, in particular, stood out from the others.

'It's identical to the golden statue you found in Teo's grave,' Gladius commented, as Decimus and Olu both nodded in recognition of the familiar statue. 'This has to be the place.'

'It's too easy,' Decimus mumbled, noticing how empty the palace grounds seemed. 'It's all too easy. Running into the old woman, our journey here – I feel like we were meant to get here – like we've been watched and guided this entire time.' He turned to the others with a warning look. 'Be careful.'

'Us?' Ruma hazarded, sarcastically. 'It was you who gave away your sword to a crone.'

Decimus smiled ruefully and, without another word, the group stealthily approached the palace gardens. They moved in a series of measured dashes. Decimus hurried forward, crouched beside a hedge to check the area and then signalled to Ruma and Gladius. They would then rush to meet up with Decimus, before repeating the entire operation, this time with Ruma at the front.

Covering the grounds with haste, they reached the edge of the palace in no time at all. As Decimus crouched beside a large door in the main building's south wall, he noticed – not for the first time – that there wasn't a single guard in sight.

'On the count of five,' he whispered, holding up a hand to illustrate the point. 'We'll open the door and sneak inside.' He raised his hand and extended a finger.

One.

Two.

Three.

Four—

He didn't get to five. Three shadows detached themselves from one of the lower roof sections and dropped, silently, to the floor. The first leapt on him and the pair went tumbling back down the steps and into the palace gardens.

Stunned by the speed of the attack, Gladius

didn't even have time to turn around before he was assailed by a second shadow. The small figure, clad completely in black from head to toe, struck out with a series of well-aimed blows, one of them, a poke to the throat which caused Gladius to wretch and gasp for breath. Beside him, Ruma was having even more trouble. The scrawny Etrurian wasn't used to meeting his match in a fight, and certainly wasn't accustomed to missing with his strikes. The first two punches he threw met with thin air, and a last-minute elbow sweep was quickly turned into a hold that nearly broke his arm. He tried to swing his knee up in an effort to catch out his opponent, but his legs were promptly kicked from under him and he landed with a painful thump on the top of the palace steps. However, a solid instinct for battle kept him moving, and he quickly provided a few surprises of his own. Rolling aside the second he hit the ground, Ruma locked both arms around the attacker's mid-section and barrelled him into the palace wall. Pinning the little figure with one hand, he drove a fist at him. Again, the blow was turned aside, and Ruma found himself flat on his back once more, this time with no idea how he'd got there.

Decimus wasn't faring any better. Either the assailant he was facing felt no pain whatsoever, or else he was so flexible that any attempt to break his arms was like trying to twist and bend treacle.

To make matters worse, the masked figure was moving so quickly that Decimus couldn't actually get a firm grip on him. When he finally did manage to snatch hold of an arm, he found himself chopped on the back of the neck with such force that he fell to the ground, stunned and shaking.

Nearby, Gladius roared with anger and frustration as he threw fist after fist at the dodging, weaving body of his attacker. He just couldn't keep up with the pace of the fight; a fact that was costing him dearly. After several attempts to corner his foe, in a rage of furious and uncontrollable exasperation, he picked up a miniature statue and hurled it in what he hoped was the general direction in which the sprightly figure was heading.

Miraculously, it caught its target on the shoulder and the mysterious attacker went down. Gladius looked to the heavens and forced his lips into a thankful smile, but it didn't last for long: to his horror, the little masked warrior leapt straight back on to his feet and cartwheeled towards him.

Three swift chops were aimed at Gladius,

who dodged one, glanced aside the other – and got hit with the third. This final assault knocked the wind from out of him, and he snatched at his throat in another attempt to find his breath. But his opponent gave him no rest: a flurry of blows floored him and he collapsed in a tired heap on the steps.

A few feet away, Ruma was being choked into

unconsciousness. He'd fought valiantly, but his attacker was smaller, faster and more determined to succeed. Nevertheless, a fighter until the end, Ruma gave almost as good as he got. Every punch was met with one of equal strength, every kick blocked or twisted. In the end, it was a single blow that felled the scrawny Etrurian. Like Gladius, he dropped his guard for a mere fraction of a second. Unfortunately, for a trained ninja, a fraction of a second was more than enough time to strike. The punch was short, sharp and driven with speed under the chin. Ruma felt the world swim, and his head suddenly seemed to weigh heavily on his shoulders. The light drifted from his eyes, and he sagged into unconsciousness.

Decimus had never fought such an opponent in all his life: not in the wilds of Campania, not in the Arena of Doom and not even in the labyrinths beneath it. The little masked combatant moved with such breathtaking speed that it was like fighting three opponents, each with their own skills and methods. He was outmatched, and he knew it. Still, the young gladiator fought on … even as he saw his friends fall and felt the two remaining warriors creep up on him. He was determined to land one strike, however ineffectual, against the wasp-like enemy he faced. All he needed was an opportunity: no one could move this fast for long.

Then he made a decision. The only way to land a blow, he thought suddenly, was to take the punches thrown at him instead of dodging them. After all, if anyone could take such punishment, it was Decimus Rex.

He straightened his chin . . . and, for the briefest of seconds, stopped dodging.

One strike: a sweeping blow to the chin. Decimus staggered, but stayed on his feet.

Two strikes: a sharp poke to the throat. Decimus coughed, spat and glared back at the warrior.

Three strikes: a flat chop, this time to the side of the neck.

Decimus didn't even feel this one. Instead, he threw the punch he'd been storing up all his energy for: a single, driving fist – not swung or brought up in a wild arc, but high and direct. It slammed straight into the warrior's head, and he fell backwards, hitting the ground with a dull thud.

Spewing a lungful of air, Decimus fought to maintain his balance after the incredible drain of the fight. He looked down.

Barely able to focus on the scene around him, he watched with bewildered awe as his floored opponent sprang back to his feet and hit him with exactly the same ferocity.

Decimus took a step back . . . and crashed to the ground in a mess of tired limbs.

The three fighters gathered together and removed their masks. Then they dragged their fallen victims to the foot of the palace steps. Maintaining a disciplined silence, they stood beside the prone gladiators and clapped their hands: once, twice, three times.

From within the palace, two figures emerged. The first was a tall, slim oriental man with long

hair, two thin moustaches, a long pointy beard
and a grizzled, almost insane look on his face.
He was dressed in a suit of pure-green armour,
and a long, curved sword hung at his side. Upon
his head, he wore an ivory crown. Two serpents
curled around the sides of the headpiece,
seemingly in the setting of a jewelled sea.
Indeed, the King of Yelang was a sight to

behold. Unfortunately, neither Decimus, Ruma, or Gladius were in any condition to view his magnificence.

As the king clapped his hands in reply to the call, his three warriors bowed before him, each

proudly presenting their prey.

The king nodded sagely, and turned his attention to the man who'd moved to join him at the top of the steps.

Slavious Doom, equally imposing in his now-familiar suit of demon-armour, returned the nod . . . and even mustered a round of applause himself.

'Your imported fighters have done well, King D'Tong,' he boomed. 'Indeed they are powerful, as your words promised.'

The King of Yelang looked at Slavious Doom and frowned deeply. 'I thank you, Doom Lord,' he began. 'But you have not kept your promise. You said to me five. Five boys to test my maze but here there are three; three only.'

Slavious Doom gave a grim nod, but his

smile did not waver.

'Fear not,' he said. 'The others will come, like rats to the bait. For now, at least, we should let the entertainment commence!'

CHAPTER III

THE

TRAP

Decimus awoke, cold. As his eyes adjusted to the light, he realized firstly that he was lodged in an upright position and, secondly, that he had very little room to move.

The light swam around him, and he felt the rush of several emotions at once: fear, frustration, helplessness and, foremost, an insane anger.

It was then that he noticed his breath was misting up in front of him in great clouds, and disappearing before his eyes.

Decimus squinted, and shook his head: he was wedged inside a glass box.

Grunting with effort, he slid his arm up the side of the container and rubbed away the mist his own breath had formed on the surface of the box, giving himself a better view.

Shifting his hand away from the glass, he saw that several air-holes had been made in the box, at head height: it seemed they wanted him alive, at least.

Decimus shook his head a second time. He still felt disorientated, and his vision was only just beginning to come properly into focus.

Then he saw the others.

Arranged around the room in a rough triangle, they each occupied their own glass boxes. Gladius still hadn't regained consciousness, while Ruma looked wide awake and incredibly furious.

The boxes were arranged at the foot of a set of marble steps that led to a raised dais covered in emeralds. Sitting atop the throne was an oriental man dressed in an impressive suit of green armour. This, he suspected, had to be the King of Yelang.

Decimus tried to swallow, and shifted slightly behind the glass. A million questions sprang into his head, but most of these faded away at the sight of the imposing figure standing beside the throne.

Even after two years, Slavious Doom was completely unmistakable. He towered over the throne at his side, his infamous demon-helm glistening in the afternoon sun. An aura of evil surrounded the man; it was almost as though he sweated pure malice.

As Gladius slowly began to move in the box opposite, Doom stepped forward with a sickening smile on his cracked lips.

'Welcome, my young friends,' he boomed. 'Welcome to Yelang.' He began to descend the steps, the king cackling excitedly behind him. 'Your host, King D'Tong, kindly provided the services of Miriki, Tekaro and Aritezu – three ninjas fresh from the shores of Japan. I think we can all agree that they showed you and your friends the true way of the warrior.'

Doom paused halfway down the steps, and shook his head in mock regret. 'I am sorry that young Teo is not here to greet you in person, but he was thoughtful enough to send me in his place. I do hope you feel suitably spoiled by your accommodations.'

Decimus tried to spit a reply, but his throat was too dry and the words failed him. Ruma and Gladius just stared up at Doom, their faces full of utter contempt and hatred.

'I must admit, I'm disappointed not to see all five of you, here,' the overlord continued, shaking his head. 'Still, I'm overjoyed to see you, Decimus Rex – my very own nemesis. Do you have any idea of the suffering, the humiliation you and your friends have caused me?'

This time, Decimus found the strength to use his voice to full effect.

'Not nearly enough,' he shouted through the glass. 'You took us from our homes, our families and you expected us to perform like animals. Well, I'm glad you suffered, Doom – you pathetic coward. What's all this for, anyway? Why the trick with Teo's message? Why didn't you just send your dumb dog guards for us back home?'

Doom smiled once again, a grin that made Decimus want to drive his head against the surface of the box.

'Haha! You'd have liked that, wouldn't you? For me to send out my soldiers, so you could show me up, once again, in front of my own men? I think not. This trap is much more satisfying. It's more of a trade, in fact. King D'Tong sells me a design for the greatest maze he has ever invented, and I supply test subjects for its grand opening. How delicious.'

At the first mention of the word 'trap', Decimus immediately shot a glance at the ceiling. There were no visible chains, spikes or holes in the eaves. Ruma and Gladius had evidently had different ideas, and both of them had twisted around in the box, trying to examine the walls outside their glass prisons.

Decimus knew the trap wouldn't come from the walls: the room was too wide and, besides, the dais had no gaps at the bottom, so the king and Doom would both have been equally at risk of harm from the trap.

'Ah!' Doom sang from the steps. 'I see you're looking around, now. It's exciting, isn't it? Knowing that at any moment the floor will quite literally be taken from beneath you?'

Decimus snarled at the overlord, and slowly looked down at his feet. The floor of the box was a sliding platform; he could tell that just by looking at it. He cursed under his breath; there were no handholds to grip inside the box and the tiny air-holes were too small to work his fingers inside. In many ways, the firm knowledge that he was about to be dropped into some unknown trap was actually worse than if he'd discovered the fact when the floor actually gave way. Naturally, Doom was aware of this strategy and was delighting in it.

'Oh, and I almost forgot,' the overlord boomed, finally descending the steps and walking into the space between the boxes. 'Do give my regards to Teo if you see him down there ...'

Doom glanced back at the king, and nodded.

Barely moving, D'Tong flicked his forefinger and depressed a concealed button on the arm of his throne.

There was no sound of any kind: no clanking, no click and no creak of shifting cogs. The floor of Ruma's box simply slid silently aside, and the scrawny Etrurian plunged out of sight.

The king clapped, Doom smiled and Gladius dropped inside his own box, his arms scrambling madly at the glass walls as he vanished from view.

Decimus glared at the smirking overlord, and took a deep breath.

'You should have walked away and forgotten about us, Doom,' he screamed through the glass. 'I'll be back, and this time no collapsing arena will save y—'

He didn't get to finish his threat.

Ruma was agile, not simply because of his size or the strength in his deceptively scrawny limbs. The Etrurian had always been quick. Even as a boy, he could run rings around the other children in his village. There was something else about Ruma and his speed: whenever he moved quickly, whether by accident or intention, he got a rush of adrenaline that made him feel glad to be alive. In his short time at the arena, he'd actually enjoyed many of the trials. He'd even felt a brief burst of excitement when he'd leapt from the top of Suvius Tower with a chain around his leg. Now, however, Ruma was not merely charged with the thrill of the ride; he was absolutely, totally, mind-numbingly terrified.

He plunged downwards at a pace he had never experienced in his life. Water sloshed all

around him as he slid down the sides of the tube he was moving along like a leaf caught in a rushing tide.

Just when Ruma succumbed to his own fear and began to scream out for his gods to save him, he flew from the end of the tube and shot across the floor of a subterranean chamber, sliding most of the way on his back. A wall of water sprayed up all around him, as he ploughed on.

'Arghgghgghghghghghghghghghghghgh!'

The gangly Etrurian was still screaming when he hit the far wall of the room and came to an abrupt halt. His last, desperate cries echoed in his new surroundings, and died away.

A few seconds passed, with only the sound of dripping water to challenge the grim silence of the chamber.

Ruma wiped some of the water from his eyes and sat up, realizing with no small amount of relief that the water in the room wasn't very high. He struggled to his feet and splashed into the centre of the room, the wash lapping around his ankles as he studied the chamber.

Far from the jagged underground cavern he'd initially expected, the room was actually an almost perfect square cut from the rock. Several exits were visible in the rough walls, and Ruma had only just noticed these when his attention was ripped away by the approaching scream echoing all around him.

Ruma looked up at the ceiling and down at the floor before he spotted two holes opposite the one he'd emerged from. These were also at ankle height, and Ruma quickly tried to work out from their position which one of his friends would arrive first. He didn't have enough time to guess, however, as at that moment Gladius exploded from the nearest hole and blasted across the floor of the chamber, sending up great plumes of water on either side of him.

Gladius slid to a grinding halt before he hit the far wall, out of breath and with his face stretched into a horrific grimace. Ruma hurried up to his friend, and attempted to help him to his feet.

'Quick! You're OK! Get up!' Ruma shouted, gripping Gladius under his heavy arms. 'We need to get out of the way before Decimus gets here!'

Gladius coughed and spluttered as he

heaved himself up and, with Ruma's assistance, staggered to the far side of the chamber.

They'd only just made it to the wall when the young gladiator's cries echoed all around them. Ruma grinned: at least all three of them had found the experience equally frightening.

'Argh-gh-gh-gh-gh-gh-gh-gh-gh-gh-gh-gh-gh-gh-gh-ggh-ggh-ghgh!'

Decimus shot out from the last hole, but unlike the others he actually flew over the water and hit the wall before he landed, knocking the air from his lungs and badly cracking his arm on the wall of the chamber.

He cried out in pain, and Ruma hurried over to him.

'Decimus! Are you OK?'

The young gladiator staggered to his feet, but his face was set in a pained frown and his arm hung loosely by his side.

'Is it broken?' Gladius asked, splashing through the water towards them.

Decimus shook his head.

'I don't think so,' he muttered. 'But – aghgh – I can't bend it.'

Ruma took hold of the arm and helped Decimus to stretch it, slightly.

'Argghhh!'

'You can't move it at all?'

'No! It's too painful: I'll just have to rest it by my side, and do without it for the time being. Where are we?'

'Underground,' Gladius said, always one to state the obvious. 'Again.'

'I've looked this room over already,' said Ruma. 'We should move.'

'Agreed.'

The three friends headed into the middle of the room, and were halfway to one of the main exits when Ruma suddenly realized they were wading.

'Hold on!' he shouted, seizing Gladius by the arm. 'This water was at ankle height when I got here.'

Decimus stared around the room, his eyes moving up and down the glistening walls. At length, he spotted a small hole in the far corner of the ceiling. It was roughly the size of a cannonball, and was steadily gushing water.

'We need to get out,' he snapped. 'This cavern is flooding, and I'm guessing we're supposed to drown down here. Move! Quickly!'

Ruma and Gladius followed him out of the

chamber, as the deadly tide began to rise.

CHAPTER IV

DROWNED!

Dashing madly from chamber to chamber, Decimus and the others were quickly coming to two very inescapable conclusions. First, the cave system was a vast maze of chambers and, second, there was no visible exit. The trio must have covered nearly half a mile of ground as they made their way through the maze, but each step was steadily slower as the tide of water rose higher and higher.

'There must be a flow hole in every room,' Ruma shouted. He had split from Decimus and Gladius in order that they might cover more ground, and was now two caves away. 'This place is filling up faster than a town well empties in the height of summer!'

'This is insane!' Gladius screamed. 'There

74

simply must be a way out!'

'Why?' Decimus muttered, still clutching his damaged arm. 'Doom wants us all dead, and this

trap makes sure it happens. Can't you understand that?'

Gladius shook his head in disbelief; he was racked with fear. 'B-but he didn't just call it a trap – he called it a maze! What sort of a maze has NO exit? That defeats the whole point!'

He hurried on, becoming increasingly frustrated with Decimus, who actually seemed to be taking his time as he moved through the caves.

'Face facts, Gladius! It's a trap. The king created it to kill, and that's what it does . . . slowly and painfully, I'd imagine.'

Now several caves away, Ruma's voice was far less audible. The others could just about hear him when he cried out to them.

'You boys better get in here, quickly! Now!

Quick! Argghghh!'

Decimus and Gladius both made a determined wade in the Etrurian's general direction. After a few steps, however, Decimus dived into the water and swam instead. He wasn't moving very fast on account of his injured arm, but he still reached the distant chamber faster than Gladius, who stubbornly refused to submerge himself (the memory of being trapped in the water trial at the arena was still too fresh in his mind).

Decimus noted, as he swung around in the water and returned to his feet, that the tide was now up to his chest.

To his astonishment, the chamber he'd entered was exactly the same as the countless others they'd waded through in the cave system.

He cast a puzzled glance at Ruma, who was staring at the rough wall of the room as if he'd seen a ghost.

'Hey!' Decimus snapped. 'Ruma! What's up? Why did you call us in here?'

Ruma slowly turned his head. 'That wall,' he said, pointing ahead of him, 'It only just came down. There was a tunnel there three seconds ago!'

'What was that?' said Gladius, finally wrestling his way into the room.

'The walls are moving,' Ruma confirmed. He cast a worried glance at his friends. 'This entire cave network is made up of moving walls. D'Tong must be controlling it from his throne room or something!'

Gladius frowned. 'How does that help us?' he

asked, momentarily at a loss.

'It doesn't,' Ruma admitted. 'In fact, it probably makes everything worse.'

The water was almost at head height. Gladius, who was always fighting his own tendency to panic, could feel it lapping at his chin.

'Right, then,' said Decimus, folding his bad arm into his soaking tunic. 'We either swim . . . or we drown.'

Without another word, the young gladiator dived under the water and swam out of the cave. In the chamber beyond, he emerged briefly and looked both ways before heading west.

'I'll take that direction,' Ruma hazarded. 'It's better that one of us finds a way out of here; there's no point in us all going together.'

The Etrurian plunged beneath the water and disappeared.

Gladius thought for a moment, and then paddled over to the cave wall. He decided to wait a few seconds, just in case it opened up again.

Decimus swam through a long, low tunnel and entered the largest room he'd yet seen in the maze. The ceiling of this room was higher than any of the others, and he knew it would be the wisest place to come to as a last resort, when water had filled the rest of the network. He took a moment to remember the combination of rooms he'd come through in order to reach the

large chamber. Then, plunging below once
more, he swam on.

Unknown to Decimus, Ruma was in a
passage that ran parallel to the large chamber
he'd stopped in. The water was now so high that
there wasn't a great deal of room between the
top of the tide and the ceiling, and Ruma found
that he had to keep taking mouthfuls of air in

the tiny spaces that still existed. To make matters worse, there was no sign of any exits in the new tunnel. He turned to swim back, but a wall slid down in front of him, blocking his path. Realizing the potential danger if he became trapped, Ruma immediately dived under the water: there was still a small gap, although the wall was juddering down at a swift rate. He kicked madly with both legs, narrowly swimming under the gap before it closed completely.

Gladius was about to give up on his suspicions and abandon the chamber when the wall section in front of him suddenly moved aside.

Hmm, Gladius thought, an alcove. But hadn't Ruma said there was a tunnel beyond?

Taking a deep breath, he swam into the tiny alcove beyond and began to explore the opposite wall surface. There were a few small holes, but nothing that would offer any sort of airspace.

Then the wall closed behind once again. Gladius turned in the water as quickly as he could, but the gap had already been sealed: he was trapped in an impossibly narrow alcove with no air and no visible means of escape.

Just when Decimus had decided things couldn't possibly get worse, they suddenly did.

Spikes.

Even through the murky water, he could see them rising from the floor and walls of the passage he was swimming along. Was there no depth of cruelty to which the mind of King D'Tong had not ventured?

Proceeding through the water as quickly as he could with only one arm to guide him, Decimus narrowly avoided the first row of pointed rocks as he tried to leave the new chamber. His rage spurred him on, and he managed to twist himself in the water and propel his body past another line of spikes. This time, however, the tips grazed his flesh, opening shallow wounds along his chest and stomach. He winced as the water carried him into the next room ... which, to his surprise, was the large chamber he'd paused in, before. The maze had to be arranged in some sort of circle, he thought. Even though it felt as if he was constantly moving onwards, he'd still ended up back in an earlier cave.

Then he saw Ruma. The gangly Etrurian was

moving through the water at an alarming rate, a look of extreme panic on his face. It was several seconds before Decimus realized exactly why his friend was moving so fast, and when he did understand, he immediately wished he didn't.

The walls in the large cave were closing in: on every side.

Gladius was also locked in a sheer panic. His hatred of enclosed spaces had combined with his memories of the water trial to convince him that he was doomed. Still, he had managed to find a tiny breathing space at the very top of the small alcove, so at least he wasn't drowning yet.

He took another great lungful of air, and

dived under the water. To his relief, the wall he'd wedged himself beyond started to shift once again. This time, however, the wall behind him moved as well. With only a second in which to make a decision, he plumped for the same tunnel that Ruma had spied earlier.

Decimus and Ruma writhed frantically in the water. The great chamber was a mass of moving walls; they closed in on every side, shrinking any possibility of evasion as they drew together ... faster ... and faster.

Sensing the end was near for both of them, Decimus stretched himself out horizontally against two of the approaching walls. He prayed to the gods that he would be strong enough to hold them apart, even for a few seconds . . . but his prayers went unanswered. The walls simply folded his limbs up, and he felt his knees being pushed up to his chin.

Beside him, Ruma had tried and failed with the same tactic, believing that the two of them might be able to produce some sort of resistance against the crushing drive of the stone. It was no good.

Their situation was hopeless.

Gladius spiralled through the water, using his weight advantage to make solid turns as the tunnel took a series of sharp lefts and rights. There was more air in these passages; they were evidently taking longer to fill with water. He soon saw the reason for this: the tunnels in this part of the maze sloped, and the downward pressure of the water had actually caved in a small section of wall at the end of the eastern passage. Had D'Tong made a critical error in his design of the maze, not realizing he should have made all the chambers level in order to assist the rise of the tide? Gladius hoped so.

Diving in the water once more, he wriggled through the collapsed section of rock and swam into the tunnel beyond.

Decimus felt his strength ebbing away as the walls of the underground chamber drew closer and closer. Ruma was now striking out wildly, kicking his legs and flailing with his arms as if the solid rock was a foe to be defeated instead of the lifeless, immovable barrier that it undoubtedly was. It didn't give an inch.

The two warriors now somersaulted over one another as the water finally overcame them.

Land! Could it really be ... actual, physical, ground!

Gladius exploded from the water and clambered up on to a bank of sliding rocks, his breath coming in fits and bursts as he collapsed on to his knees, thanking the gods in their great mercy for sparing him.

He took several further deep gulps of air and then looked around at the new area in which he found himself. Sadly, the rock bank was a dead-end ... but it must have been mined at one point or another because a wooden prop supported the ceiling and a large and very rusty pickaxe had been wedged in the opposite wall at an odd angle.

Gladius looked from the pickaxe to the prop, and back again. Then he staggered over to the wall.

What have I got to lose, he thought to himself. Either I get crushed to death ... or I drown.

The big youth reflected on his trial in the sewer beneath Arena Primus, and put a firm grip on the pickaxe handle.

Decimus and Ruma were drowning.

Forced together like fish caught in a net, their limbs slowly stopped moving. They hung in the water, suspended in the silent, drifting murk, the last few bubbles escaping their tired lips as the water consumed them.

The pickaxe was so heavy that even Gladius, whose considerable size made him an ideal wielder, was hard pushed to get enough momentum in the small cave. Still, after several practice swings, he struck the wooden prop and was pleasantly surprised when it bit into the middle of the support. There was a satisfying crack as the wood began to splinter, and Gladius repeated the action twice. On the third

stroke, the prop gave way completely. There was
a brief collapse of rock above, and then silence.

Gladius threw down the pickaxe, and waited.
In the stillness of the watery cave, the only
audible sound was his own ragged breath.

Well, he thought, at least now I know it wasn't holding up anything particularly important.

Then a sudden, distant rumble signalled that he was wrong.

Very wrong.

The rumble grew steadily louder, and louder, and louder ... until it was a deafening roar.

Gladius tried to remember everything he'd learned about cave-ins from the miners who'd visited Brindisium when he was a boy. He made for the widest part of the passage, but quickly realized that this would mean re-entering the water. Unfortunately, there didn't seem to be any other alternative ...

It was then that Gladius got a nasty shock that he would remember for the rest of his life. Everything he'd ever learned about the collapse of mining caves told him to watch out for the ceiling. Nobody had said anything about watching out for the floor.

In a crushing, tumbling, roar of rock, the floor gave way on Gladius, followed quickly by the walls and most of the ceiling. With the removal of just a single prop, Gladius had inadvertently brought down the entire cave network.

Ruma and Decimus were breathing their last, desperate gasps when a large hole appeared in the basin of the cave they were drowning in. The effect was like a plug being pulled, and a swirl of water sucked them both into its created

funnel. The two young fighters went down ...
down ... down into the dark.

Semi-conscious and still in a state of shock,
Gladius flowed along a new waterway far below
the caves. Rocks, dirt and mud zoomed past
him as more and more of the maze fell apart.
Gladius was carried left, right and left again,
diverted along a new intersection in a series of
slippery, sliding, long-forgotten shafts.

Then there was light; nothing more than a
glimmer at first, but brightening with every
new turn in the tunnel.

Gladius was carried further and further ...
faster and faster ... until he emerged into fresh

rushing air and bright blinding daylight.

For the briefest of seconds he fell like a bundle of rags through the air. Then the gushing waters of the immense waterfall consumed him. He plunged an impossible, death-defying distance and hit the lagoon at the base of the waterfall, like a great boulder dropped into a pond.

Far above him, their lungs still heavy with the pressures of the smothering tide, Decimus and Ruma burst out of the high cave and plummeted after him.

They had escaped the king's dreaded water maze ... but at what cost?

COMING SOON

Having escaped King D'Tong's dreaded water maze, Decimus and the others become more determined than ever to find out the truth about Teo. However, before the group can mount any kind of search, they must reach Argon and Olu on the coast of China. This in itself will not be easy, as the evil king has dispatched his three dreaded ninjas to bring the trio back . . . dead or alive.

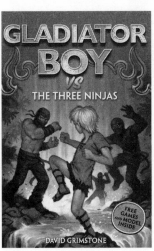

THE THREE NINJAS

GLADIATOR GAME
THE MAZE

In this two-player game, one person takes on the role of King D'Tong, while the other plays Decimus Rex.

HOW TO PLAY

The player playing King D'Tong closes his eyes and jabs a pencil at the symbols grid on pages 106-107. If the pencil tip lands on a square containing his character's symbol (the jewel) he may start first. If he lands on Decimus's symbol (the sword), the other player begins instead.

If King D'Tong goes first, he immediately plays the grid once more. Regardless of the symbol this time, he checks the number result and may close

THAT many walls along the level 1 line. If this blocks off EVERY exit (i.e he hits a 4), the game is immediately over and King D'Tong wins!

If Decimus goes first, he immediately plays the grid once more. Regardless of the symbol this time, he checks the number result and may move Decimus forward THIS many levels.

On his next turn (or first turn – depending on who plays first) King D'Tong will then close off the exits on whichever level Decimus has reached.

Play continues in turn, until either Decimus's route has been blocked or he reaches the line of escape! King D'Tong needs to throw a four to block off Decimus's escape. Can he do it before Decimus hits enough numbers to cross all the levels and escape the maze?

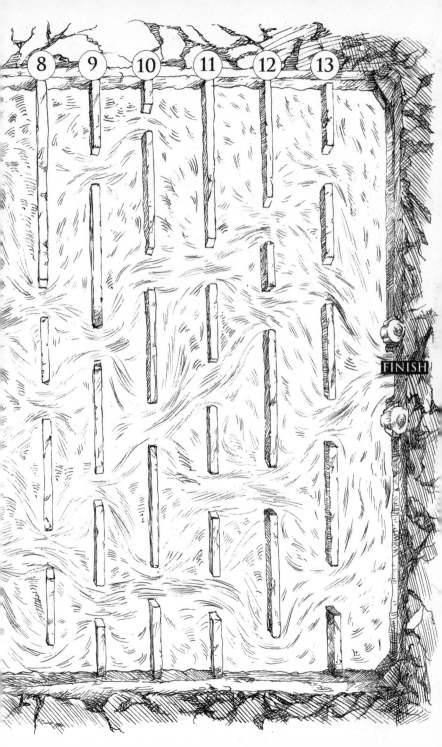

SEARCH GRID

1 💎	2 🗡	4 💎	3 🗡	2 🗡	3 💎	2 🗡	4 💎	1 🗡	1 💎	4 🗡	2 💎
2 💎	2 🗡	1 💎	1 🗡	1 💎	1 🗡	2 💎	3 🗡	4 💎	4 🗡	3 💎	1 💎
1 🗡	1 💎	4 🗡	2 💎	1 🗡	3 💎	2 🗡	2 💎	1 🗡	2 💎	1 🗡	1 🗡
1 🗡	2 💎	1 🗡	1 🗡	1 💎	2 🗡	4 💎	3 🗡	2 🗡	3 🗡	2 💎	4 💎
2 🗡	3 💎	2 🗡	4 💎	1 🗡	1 💎	4 🗡	2 💎	1 🗡	3 💎	2 🗡	2 💎
1 💎	1 🗡	2 💎	3 🗡	4 💎	4 🗡	3 💎	1 💎	1 🗡	2 💎	4 💎	3 🗡
1 🗡	3 💎	2 🗡	4 💎	2 💎	1 🗡	3 💎	3 🗡	2 💎	2 🗡	1 💎	1 🗡

SEARCH GRID

3	2	2	1	2	1	1	1	2	4	3	2
2	4	3	2	3	2	4	1	1	4	2	1
2	1	1	1	1	2	3	4	4	3	1	1
1	4	2	1	3	2	2	1	2	1	1	2
1	2	1	1	2	4	3	2	3	2	4	1
2	3	2	4	1	1	4	2	1	3	2	2
1	3	2	2	1	2	1	1	1	2	4	3

CHARACTER PROFILE
KING D'TONG

NAME: King D'Tong

FROM: Yelang, Han Dynasty – China

HEIGHT: 1.85 metres

BODY TYPE: Lean, muscular

Fact File:
* King of Yelang.
* Inventor of the dreaded water maze.
* Has three ninja servants: Miriki, Tekaro & Aritezu.

KING D'TONG QUIZ: How well do you know King D'Tong? Can you answer the following three questions?

1. WHAT COLOUR IS THE KING'S ARMOUR?

2.WHAT IS THE NAME OF THE KING'S HOME?

3. WHAT FACIAL HAIR DOES KING D'TONG HAVE?

Answers: 1. Green, p.49 **2.** The Winter Palace, p.35 **3.** Two moustaches and a pointy beard, p.49

HOW MANY OF

GLADIATOR BOY

SERIES TWO HAVE YOU COLLECTED?

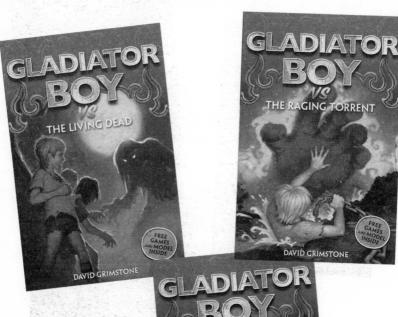

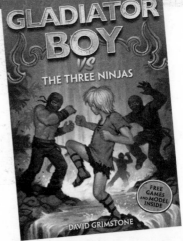

GLADIATOR BOY
VS
THE INSANE FURY

DAVID GRIMSTONE

FREE
GAMES
AND MODEL
INSIDE

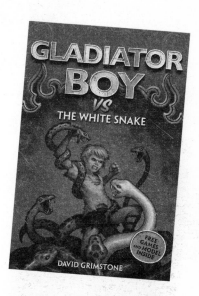

GLADIATOR BOY
VS
THE WHITE SNAKE

DAVID GRIMSTONE

FREE
GAMES
AND MODEL
INSIDE

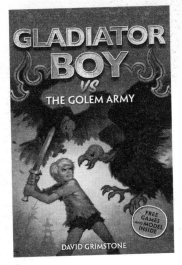

GLADIATOR BOY
VS
THE GOLEM ARMY

DAVID GRIMSTONE

FREE
GAMES
AND MODEL
INSIDE

GLADIATOR BOY

WWW.GLADIATORBOY.COM

Have you checked out the Gladiator Boy website?
It's the place to go for games, downloads,
activities, sneak previews and lots of fun!

Sign up to the newsletter at
WWW.GLADIATORBOY.COM
and receive exclusive extra
content and the opportunity
to enter special members-only
competitions.

cut along the lines

C

B

A

X

cut along the lines

cut along the lines   Y

GLADIATOR BOY

WWW.GLADIATORBOY.COM

Cut out the character and arena section
along the black lines.
Using the instructions opposite make
your own Chinese combat wall.

Hodder
Children's
Books

GLADIATOR
BOY
WWW.GLADIATORBOY.COM

Hodder
Children's
Books